THE CURSE OF ANDREWMENT VILLAGE

THE CHANGE OF DEAD SOUL

SUMEET KUMAR

ISBN 979-888530914-1

Sumeet Kumar

Sumeet Kumar, A adult who experiences many phases of love in his life , get broked many times , stands up everytime and keep moving to the next phases of the life. In reality he is a writter as well as singer (as a hobby). Very exciting and interesting fact about him is that he is a author of New era i.e. he starts his journey of writing at the age when he was going to schools to get the study.

His some famous works i.e. Maturity Of Love (Genre - Love), Privacy For Dream (Genre - Middle Class), Army Squad of Love (Genre- The Seperation of Army Love), 5 Days of Love (Genre- Temporarily Love), Th e Endearment Of Love (Genre - Historical Era Of Love), Social Destruction Indo-Pak (Genre - The Story of The Love At The Time Of Division Of India And Pakistan), Middle Class Soul (Genre - The Dreams of Middle Class), The Accursed Kanatpur (Genre - The Horrific Story Of A Village), Wrong Number (Genre - The Suspenseful Physco Killer Story), The Secrecy Of Deadly Midnight (Genre - The Suspense About a Crime), Fragile Religious Of Death (Genre- The Death Of A Trustful Person), Nature Vs Science (Genre - The Future Battle Between Nature And Science In A Horrific Way), Generic Man (Genre - The Dream of I.I.T), The Unconsious 12 Hours (Genre - The Illusion At Stage Of Comma), The Strange Burden (Genre - The Burden Of Love) , Her Existence (Genre - The Femlae Pain In The Society) , Jockstrap Prize (Genre - The True Story Of A National Athlete). are available on various geners on the offcial platform of **Amazon, Flipkart and Notionpress**. You can buy them from there.

Contents

PREFACE

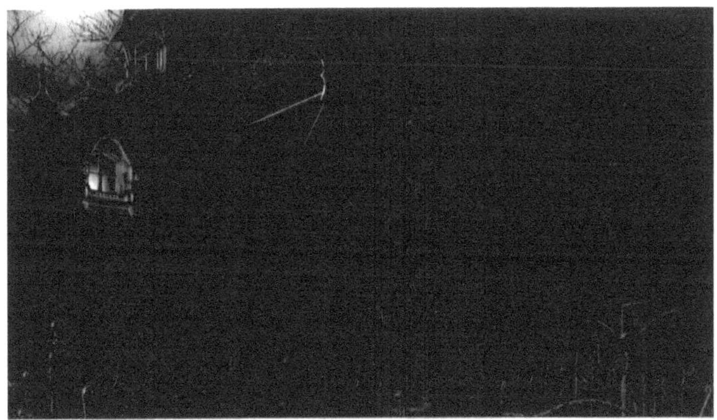

THE CURSE OF ANDREWMENT VILLAGE

These days the world of blind faith is everywhere in the world because people take the arrival of small things to the goddess society (as you must have seen in most of the temples that sometimes our stone-made Nandi starts drinking milk, sometimes I have also heard that Tulsi's plant is flourishing, it is a matter of which any plant only observes because it is needed. But not all of us, even with some superstition, we give the form of goodess krishna and I want to say a thing there is no other work for the tiger who will come every year to promote us and if human beings are not able to handle them in the world then how will we take care of them, it is a matter of thinking. If only humans have to believe. Believe in the unity that exists between them and move them forward, but it can't happen to us. Friendship and love is his trust . Because nowadays soul is enough to become one's own habit.

ITS OKAY
TO TRUST
SOMEONE
BUT NOT MORE
THAN
YOURSELF

Acknowledgements

Aman Kumar

Special Thanks to **Aman Kumar** who worked so hard in the preparation of this book. He has continually put with my passi ve voice, omission of words, and late night calls. You have be en wonderful. Thanks to him for his precious time in reviewing proposals , individual chap ters and early drafts, along with his suggestions on the applicability of the material to the world.

• x •

Prologue

We have heard a lot of ghost stories in childhood, but no one has ever seen them. Because they show more in our imagination if not in films. In childhood, our parents are afraid of many things by saying that they do not Know that there is a ghost who will eat you, sometimes even by saying that if you do not eat food, then you will be taken away after getting a ghost and after a while after listening to those things, we used to eat food too. Somewhere in the world today it has become a business for the people to run away from the ghost. If someone has done something abnormal in the house, then first of all, the family members think that the shadow of some ghost. Take Baba to the fakir. If a child is not able to eat, then people also tell him that it is the shadow of some witch or witch or ghost, due to which he cannot eat food. Sometimes we attack someone in a deserted house at night What tea we see, we declare it haunted (ghostly) house within a few days and after that, far from going to him, we sometimes come in front of him by mistake. So as if it seems that your soul is somewhere different and your body is different.. in childhood, have seen many films, that too during the day because I never dared to see it at night and even if I had seen it by mistake, it would have been the whole night. when we see some bad imagination then we thought in the dream and because of that sleep would have been bad and the next day would have been bad because of her. The school continued and we never used to go on time, due to which the teacher used to make us stand on the ground. Give. Today, in every accessory (villages) one gets to hear the story of some ghost. This news is sure to be defeated because a ghost lives in the feet of the banyan tree. The bonding of ghosts is also very good with tree because most of these two names are flour and I think there is a very good relationship between both of them because most of the ghosts make their home on tree. I have heard that I have not heard. Well all this is a matter of coincidence and till the time it is true, only gardeners know. Everyone in the world has to do something practically, even if it is some science. Sari things people want to see practically now and do it too. Reality is not what is seen all the time, there is also reality which can be heard by the particles sometimes... Well all these are just batons and behind them there is a lot of shame. Those who have ever seen them... I also tell to tell such a story which is true to a large extent, say that it is not a story but a snake (cursed) in which he has imprisoned some Kiruh even today. Has kept in his arms . a soul who has sacrificed himself in front of death because of you and did not dare to say a word... She..... I have heard some sari rumours, listened to many sarcastic stories like (the sound of someone squeaking in the library room of the school is heard in the night, sometimes there is some noise) If he has been closed for a long time, then he also sometimes considers him as the house of ghosts and also calls him by the name of Bhoot Bungalow, then look at the story somewhere in the forest, that too there is a discussion of ghosts all the time (I feel that sometimes there are no ghosts) It will be politics that has only one place but its voice is everywhere .

I
The Curse

The Beginning of Curse dates back to 1940, where there was a sehar between two rivers, whose name was Andrewment, its beauty was such that any woman would fall in love upon seeing it, there was a big pahar and greenery everywhere and there was no such sehar in comparison to it. Who could compete with its beauty, in this sehar the rule of two castes castes .. on one side were Brahmins and on the other and Rajputs. In this city, both the castes and the castes below them used to live in a lot of water, that is, sometimes with anyone. No mat perforation and no showing anyone down or taking advantage of his rule .. Perhaps this was also the reason why Andrewment was so beautiful .. that even the animals did not harm any human race, they all got along well with them Used to live .. whenever festival came, I used to have such decorations in Andrewment, I have some heaven and the human here should be the form of a god and the women should be the symbol of a nymph. 20th July, 1980, when everyone is enjoying happiness but some There were also people who were in a hurry to damage Andrewment. defined (they say that there is no evil, that evil also comes). The best statue of him was a Rajputana sword Tijiska the whole part was made only of diamonds and the second place was also a book of brahmins which was made entirely of gold .. that rajputs and brahmins believed that both of them should stay in usually Andrewment to be beautiful and the best ..

But some robbers were trying to steal the sword of rajputana, it was the night of Basant Panchami, everyone was asleep in city, then the robbers planned to steal her and somehow went to my night while hiding in Kantapur but they do not know this. It was believed that a man could pick up the sword and the book could be picked up by a true brahmin or a true Rajput. Gone, because I had said earlier also that the animals here also live well with the human race and also help each other, when someone saw the robber stealing, the voice echoed in the whole sehar that some robbers came who were our porcupines. The Sword and the Book of Our Books They are trying to shove, then what was the whole cities peoples are asleepon that time after hearing their voice the robbers also tried to run away but they could not run because if someone touches the male porcupine sword then his soul gets imprisoned in the temple itself .. He probably did not know this, at that time, soon after that he reached the whole city and all the robbers he had beaten and killed. He had received this knowledge by going to the place, so he used to steal, but never got caught. .. Vaisheyska name was probably an attack, on the day he was planning to return, then the attacker explained to him many times that we should not steal in this sehar because it rains in this sehar. From Rajputana and Brahmin the priests were guarding the sword and the book and it is difficult to go inside the temple but the rest of his companions still did not agree and finally they chose the day of Basant Panchami to steal .. everyone that that day but It happened in the fire of Basant Panchami and vikrant did not die because when he died, the people of city thought that they should be done .. At the time, they did not know that the attacker had not died yet, he was only intoxicated for a while, and his stories It is still going on .. But by the time the people of city came to know about it, it was too late .. Their body was engulfed in flames and their body had turned into ashes, but even then the attacker was still alive. In the end, it was burnt only when his body was caught on fire, then he would shout loudly, save, but by the time it was so much fire that his whole body was engulfed, only the eyes and tongue were safe .. Then at that time he said something like this Since this day, there has never been any happiness nor any festival made in Andrewment .. People in Andrewment did not know that the attacker of time is such a magician or he knows such an illusion that will take the happiness of their pureseher to China at the same time .. when When he was saved, half of his life was burnt, but his mother-in-law was still walking. It was only then that he cursed in a human condition, which he could not even imagine. You will become the reason and the beauty of which Kanatapur is famous, that beauty will be a curse for this sehar (courses will remain .. and that sword, and the books of that book, all that is your symbol, will become the reason for the destruction of this city, and your ancestors) Those who protect you will be the reason for the destruction of your genetics .. .. After a few days, he was cursed, the attacker had died on the happy day but his soul was still wandering everywhere there was a happiness but aftrer few day in the city there was a destruction and The reason was...

II

The Evil Eye

A few days after the death of the akrant Curse become Poison , Andrewment had gone to the deserted place where there was a noise of happiness, now it started to be a noise of mourning. For the sake of each other, first they used to deal with their lives to save each other, now they were making a deal of death to kill each other. Because whenever the man kept a foot in the temple, this man tried to touch the sword, that sword would become the cause of death of vikrant. He was imprisoned, due to which he was forced to take someone's life. In the jest, the people used to see the beauty of it coming from Distance, now no one used to tell him to come but the people who do not get tired of praising the people, now the same people are different about its cursed. Started making different conversation. There were reasons and symbols of it, now they became the reason for the epidemic of city. complete city became a problem in a few days everywhere bash was being made everywhere only the noise of crying children was being made to kill some human. And the Rajputana said that we should keep the sword and the book of books somewhere else from the male temple, due to which the death of the people passing through it should be done. Despite wanting, he used to pass through and many times he even tried to get him locked up but all the time he only had to face death and within a few days a door sat in the people of the service, so because of which someone would leave his house. Not only were there Rajputana and Brahmin belonged to the same, so now the elder Brahmin realized that we have to do a big worship and without reason. His soul will have to be imprisoned and our ancestors will have to be freed from treachery, but he was not aware of the teaching that no one can imprison his soul because only salvation and his will is the only solution, which is the first victim of his whole life again. He got the big havans done, the big prayers done, yet the soul of the attacker was so strong that he could not imprison him, after that he moved to Shapur, where the first big people murders were started, the curse started hunting the children too. The peoples had started killing their own children, went to the food and drink facility in complete Andrewment. Then after all this the peoples slowly started crushing the male city and within a few days, Andrewment was deserted, he started rusting in the palaces of him. Now all the animals and the feet of the plants started becoming infuriated. Half of them became empty in a few months. Bash the children, some Rajputs and some Brahmins, because that whole city was made by their ancestors. Now even winning were the remaining peoples, they too slowly started coming in the grip of drought and sometimes they were on their own. ancestors himself did not want to cause him to die. Those who had not gone to church city, they had only two. The first was that they should go to another city, where their death was happening due to the curse of the attack. He should not be. The second was to surrender his soul to him, due to which death can easily be found . It was very difficult for him to choose both of them because he neither wanted to die nor did he want to destroy his soul. Time The condition of the past started getting worse, now Andrewment had gone completely barren, every land had become barren due to which there was neither anything to eat nor anything to drink, all the ponds were dried up. And the little girl who helped her next. city was the community, now they also stopped helping, thanks to them, they started feeling that some robbers should not be caught in city., after all they all had only one living that Misra was teaching himself in some other city by cursed city. Go away to avoid the curse. Surrey went to live in city..and his elders started to think that he had escaped from the cursed The orgy of death has not stopped yet it will complete............

*"***Body is burned ,***
but my soul is still there in them

*and what did you think
that the journey of your pain is just till this time,
look back and see the whole universe is still
there............"*

III

Calmness Of Soul

After a few days, when the logs started dying slowly, everyone left Andrewment and everyone started to feel that now we have been saved from his curse (Kursed) but it was not at all, I had told earlier also. The soul of the keeper did not let them stay . and the people who had left Andrewment also started dying slowly, later whatever breeds of Rajput Brahmins they were doing slowly, they all ended. There were only a few Brahmins and Rajputs left, whose condition was not good . They thought that we should try only a newspaper and we should also try to free Andrewment from the soul of the invader . Then I found a way out of surprise . of . was his . love for his sister-in-law and it was this unity due to which he was not getting salvation even after wanting the soul of the aggressor, because he was the shade that the anger of his lover should also go with him. People did not know at that time that settlement is the reason due to which Andrewment can be again like before and free from curse was also the time of . 1980, Or Andrewment was completely deserted only then British . British . thought why not we have this whole Put Andrewment in your bass and make different types of factories here . Feet they did not know that the entire Andrewment has been imprisoned by the attacker's soul and even if they had known the memory, they would not have believed in all things . them too Knew that the porcupine sword of Rajputs and Brahmins, which is to be made of priest, and the book of scriptures which is made of gold, its famous is in the whole country . then he gave visa to his two soldiers Stephen and Richardson to inhale . which is of qualified status. Soldiers were in the same condition that was already happening with the people of Andrewment . . . It had been a long time due to which the British government was very worried about our When two soldiers left, they didn't come back yet .. That's when the resident of Kanpur, who was working, said that the government does not know that whoever goes to Andrewment never comes back .. He asked him that what is it that whatever he goes to Andrewment, he never comes back. Today we are forced to do this service like homeless: wandering undefine d Earlier the beauty of Andrewment was more than heaven, its people lived very happily and with brotherhood, and one curse has left the entire curse of Andrewment as a deserted ruin and nothing, so I request you that you too If you stay away from Sehar, it is all good, otherwise you should not be in the grip of the condition that complete Andrewment is passing through today. You are making a pretense (drama .) in front of us to save Andrewment, due to which the sword of Rajputour Brahmins can also be saved and also the texts. After that the governor said that nothing like this happens, you are speaking lie Even he tried to understand the governor for a long time, yet the governor did not listen to him and ordered the soldiers that Jake should find out what is the truth and why Stephen and Richardson have not returned yet. After that the whole of the British soldiers A hypnot (group) he went. After that a lot of time passed, no news of care came (Gov. The runner was now beginning to feel that whatever he had said is not true. When everyone took only defeat, then at last the governor thought that now I will have to go and get the right sword books from him. After that the governor also trembles upon hearing what happened with him.

IV
Reprisal Of Past

When the Governor (British Head) had just stepped into Andrewment that the whole sky was blue, the winds stopped, it became dark all around and only the sounds of crying were coming from everywhere. The Governor was very scared seeing him. When he was gone, he thought that it is right to stop, I will have to leave from here soon. (Maybe one thing will not be known but the biggest enemy of the attacker was the governor. The governor tried a lot to get him out, but his steps were not healing from one place to another. It seemed that someone holding his body from behind. Then in front of him would come the soul of the invader, which had been forged with blood. The river was flowing. That's when he asked the governor that who should be able to digest me, because of . power, even the governor's voice was not coming out) I am here today because of you, otherwise we would have been happy with your family today..after that In a low voice, the governor said that forgive me, even after winning, I had done atrocities on you, for that then vikrant said that if you did not do this with me for the rest of the time. Had I done so, I would not have lived in this condition today, the people of Andrewment would never die, nor would I ever become a robber and my spirit would keep wandering. I could not leave you alive . Can never leave for whatever you did to me. .His buds suddenly cut off both his hands and legs, he badly scratched his eyes and completely wet his whole tongue and broke all the bones that were left in the body, after that his soul himself I was imprisoned in... He had completed his revenge. There were still some other people on Governor , due to which his soul was not ready to leave Andrewment. Even after that many other people came and everyone had the same condition. Andrewment was with the people and with the governor. The attack was not a bad person, he also has many such things which neither you know nor the people of Andrewment had some condition due to which he chose the path of robber and today a soul like Bane is avenging his death from everyone. After the killing of his governor, the complete british government thought that who should only save the whole city. be destroyed with the help of arood and capture (capture) the entire sehar . The whole of the British had taken the thought that they would ruin the whole city, the spirit of revolution did not allow this to happen. they used many different weapons to defeat the soul of vikrant , even then he did not even shake a word of Andrewment because all the attacks he did would come back on him later. Due to which almost thousands of his soldiers died. After this The British government had also thought that it is really someone who is letting us go inside the wall of Andrewment . then after a few days the whole British government left from it. Hearing his condition, everyone was so hung up that no soldier said, no matter whether he belongs to any country, he did not dare to step out of the gate of Andrewment. They all now knew that the only way to go is that his Inviting death . After many years No country or any human race has stepped in .

"You are the source of my veins;
And also the opponent of my desire;
And I used to love to love you
Some wonderful moments did not allow me to fall in love
with you"

V
Pinpointing A Soul

It is said that love is such a thing that gives life to the dead as well I do not know. (Perhaps Gaya Bilatpur) The agrant was the eldest in the house, below him, he had two siblings. started doing his work like his father, but Akrant's father did not want his beta to become like him, he wanted him to be a doctor like his mother and help everyone. That's why he sent him from village to out side Andrewment to study. He was sent, but when the profession of the clothe was not working enough, then he got help from the Rajputs and from the Brahmins. Asked and he helped but at one point he would have to keep his all properties with them and would have to fight the rent from time to time. If he is gone, he will be of no benefit to him, Father, from this) . Happy time, his father told him that I do not say that you should be a simple farmer like me whose death is only a tax for everyone. Because he did his surgery in the name of Rajputo Brahmins. And after some time passed only then the attacker fell in love with a daughter of Brahmins whose name was ishwar there was a girl whose marriage was already fixed in Rajputana's house. (It was the custom of every Rajput girl to marry Brahmins and Brahmin girls in Rajputanu) but the unknown who was infatuated with the teachings fell in love with her, but the result would be very bad, perhaps she did not know this. She used to visit her every day. Look at the side everyday but never know because bramhans daughter and Akrant belonged to a very low caste (belong) that's why he never dared to go near her and the only thing was that he could not back down from his duty which was to teach him..when he asked him to speak Her father's grief kept roaming around her all the time. But in love, every bond breaks every wall. Why her father was the eldest brahmin among and he had a lot of respect in Andrewment. (Ishwar was brought up with a lot of love in his childhood, so he never goes against his family. Ask some questions. God's marriage was fixed in a Rajputana house in childhood itself and the name of her husband was Chandraprakash Rajputa, who was the son of Raja Maldev Amit Rathore Rajput (Son). Even at that time there was a British rule, due to which the Governor and Rajputana used to have a lot of relations with each other and kept going there because they were also very good friends. One thing Kedar Hans to the attacker: If I had expressed my love in front of God, I would have said The Rajputs came to know about it without saying that, is dead and his father also took a loan from him for his studies and he also had his birth, due to which he wanted to keep his heart silent for a long time. .. like every day another day also when he went to see God then at that time the watchman saw him and asked who is yum and what are you doing here .. at first he stopped talking that the society was not coming that What did he say to him, the great Brahmins of then there came who was also the father of God, they recognized him (identified) and said that you are the son of then kishan Rao, who has given his entire land to us to study you. And what are you doing? Ho..(Then the attacker replied that father had asked to ask you out of the rent, I had gone to your house in Ishliye but you were male and female. Why were not then someone told that you will come here because I have come. By the way, let me tell you that the college in which Ishwar used to study was of h father, so Akrant said . No no no you tell bash when to pay the rent, I will go after that . Seeing the attacker in a very hurry, he also went to think that what is the matter Joey is in such a hurry, after that he told him about the rent and in a while He left from that ...) After that he did not show for a long time. Then after a month he went again and on this day he finally said his word. For the attacked due to love because she accepted that when the time came, she could present her love like a fraud in front of the rest of the world..

**"You memories includes funny moments
which became the reason of smile to my face
But the enmity happened with us**

Gives the Continuous Love to our deception.""

VI
Maligant Affection

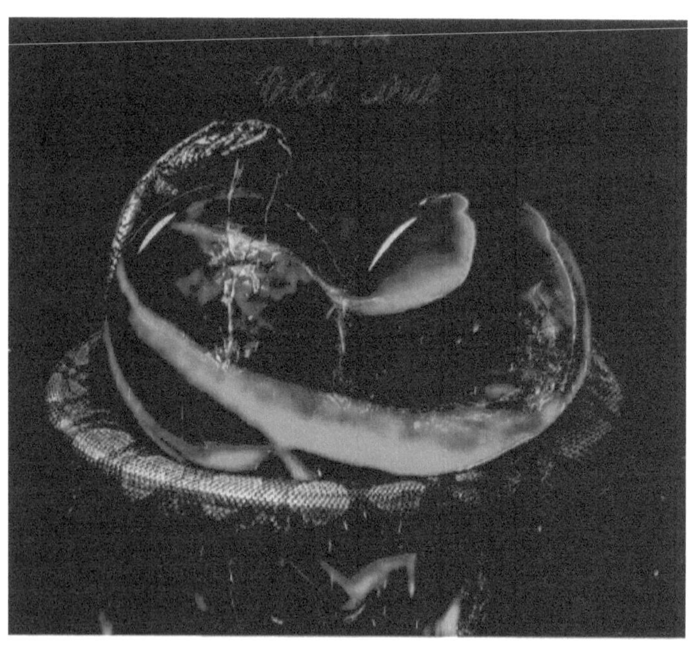

On this day God has attacked the attacker, so the sword is not a love but a hoax. The attacker did not know this even at the time of his death. Every time the attacker would come to meet him everyday, Bash would remember him, he was not entitled to anything, what the world Think what the Brahmins would do when they came to know, what would this Rajput do, he was so lost in the shadow of God's love that he could not even see his duty in front of him and to achieve the goal his father worked so hard. Maybe he had forgotten it too.

"

"Love is such an enmity
In which God takes
something from us that we loves most."

He lost his destination very soon, when he had loved God, now he had only one life, which he did not even have later. She is not called brave. It was that the entire life of the invader was with him, and that was also with him. The same thing happened when one day he went to mine again with Aakrant ,ishvara, then one of the Brahmins had seen them together and soon Bad bramhan and Rajputs came to know about this but at the time they only had credibility because they knew the invader that he would ever Can't do this. Then he himself thought that until I see with my own eyes, I will not trust him. After that, the truth on which complete knathpur was only able to see them together again turned into confidence. After that, he was called to Rajput assembly and asked if you love God. He simply said straight. When this question was asked to God, he made it plainly. Hearing this, he was shocked to hear this, what he was saying to God that this time is not for any joke, tell God what is true. Even then he said that this I was forced to make love if I do not believe that I will kill you. Hearing this, the hurt that the attacker got. No one could feel the hurt corner, nor could anyone express it . after that he also knew That with whom he fell in love was just a hoax and nothing else. He didn't say a word to him, nor is he speaking this truth of his side in front of anyone and in truth. It is not defeated because even then the attacker would have been defeated. If love is one sided, it loses two sided, it is the one who has tried to win... Nor did he fall in his own eyes because he knew that today his entire family is in danger because of his love. Rathore could have given the death sentence at a happy time but he did not want to prove himself cruel in front of complete assembly and it was not a big deal in his life that lower caste had fallen in love with a girl of an upper caste. He left the attacker at the young time from the driver . and at the young time only punished him that you have to leave the murderer. But a few days later, when Kranti was preparing to go to his side, God came to meet and said that I am sorry. Do it, father told me that if I do not speak, he will kill you, because I did not want to refuse your love at the time. Please forgive me. Said that you are afraid, we will go far away from each other . So the society did not find that God did not come for him, but he was sent by his father and Rajputs..

But what is the purpose of sending it, it will be known in the next part .

VII

The Riddle Of Demise

On the busy day, he was waiting for God to come out of Sehar's deaf as soon as he came and God did come. But what happened after that. He used to celebrate every one of them and whatever Raja maldev told him to do, he would have done it soon. In the eyes of the British and the people of city, he was a real killer, but in the eyes of King Maldev, he was a treacherous man. She made Akrant the killer of God, due to which the whole of Andrewment should believe that he had killed God because he had rejected his love in complete assembly. But this death was also very much a farce which was a big brahmin and king Maldev and His son had thought very cleverly to kill Akrant. After that, King Maldev sent his faithful to the place where God was already waiting for the invader to run away. The faithful attacked Ishwar and he started running towards city at stage speed and loudly shouted . After listening to the attack of the daughter of the Brahmin, he became very angry and without looking back, he too ran away from her..... After that the whole person became angry and he also felt that the attacker had killed the elder brahmin's daughter. Ishwar has been killed. K burnt in his own house so that everyone would feel that it was an accident (Incident) while the sisters of the attacker were alive, seeing her parents brother sister burning, she started crying loudly till anyone could hear her voice before. The governor had heard their voice and before the whole house burnt down, the governor went inside and shot both of them with his gun on his head. Due to which he also gave up his life in front of his family.... The [complete family] broke a trap in the aftermath, but their souls were still alive in some or the other encroachment, which was only and only for justice. After all, after about 2 months, the attacker came to know that now the provoked family is not in the world. I am not, he also used to say to kill himself, he did not see any hope of being alive, everywhere only his family's friends were there, they had faces and the childhood of their own brothers was visible, the sisters were smiling and seeing something. Then after a few months, he joined the army of a robber, where the chieftain was very intelligent and he also used to have a lot of hypnotizing, when he told his whole story to Sardar Inderjal Singh, then he told him why he is sad. We are the only children with you, today our family was afraid of society. Dardar Indrajal Singhkrit was like his son, so he taught his primary mantras to the victim before killing himself..... (I must be sure that this thinking is being born Why did the Sardar take the initiative before dying? After all, the Sardar died? When did it happen? In the same way, he gave his death charge to the attacker. Now why did he die, it is a mystery till today, but let's see this thing ahead, let's see .

THE EDGY

It seemed to everyone that God had died on this day but not on this day God was alive, it was just a drama that was composed by the great brahmin, King Maldev, his son and God himself. It was known that ishwara is still alive, he has not died, nor was the death of his family an accident. What was the matter..if God didn't die then he is still there and why is he not in Andrewment Sent him and why he wanted the right sword and the books of the scriptures really he only wanted this don thing for himself, this someone was behind it, and he sent his soldiers saying that you go and bring the book and sword of the gland. If he says, he himself could have made himself happy with Rajputs, this from Brahmins. Then why is it like this... Click here and wait for the next part............

"

"some fun moments are here with me still now
with the desire is enough
But demand of desires is still left in the
present...."